Published 2015 by Mariposa Blanca Publishing, LLC
1103 Stein Street, Lafayette, Colorado, 80026 U.S.A.
303-955-4817

Distributed by Satiama, LLC
www.satiama.com

ISBN: 978-0-692-54362-7 Library of Congress Control Number: 2015916062

Story by Arnold Bustillo
Written and Illustrated by Susan Andra Lion
Book Design by Susan Andra Lion
Editing by Karen L Stuth, Satiama Writers Resource

PRINTED IN CHINA

Mariposa
Blanca
PUBLISHING, LLC

White Butterfly
and Her Wings of Many Colors

Story by Arnold Bustillo

Written and Illustrated by Susan Andra Lion

DEDICATION

To Gilma Bustillo, we love you.

ACKNOWLEDGMENTS

Thanks to my wonderful family and friends for their support
and encouragement to bring my dad's story to the world.

Thank you, Dad, for your many gifts and for the special gift
of this beautiful story. I love you.

And to my loving husband Paul — without you, Mariposa
Blanca Publishing and this book would never have been born.

In the Garden of Fragrance, in the remote village of Everbloom, there lived a sparkling white butterfly. Her beauty and strength made her special, but what made her most remarkable was her generous heart and her ability to heal. She won many friends by using speed and flying tricks to divert an enemy's attention so the smaller creatures could fly to safety. White Butterfly was the greatest flying entertainer in the land. She amazed and astounded others with her acrobatic flying, first ascending to the sun, then rapidly swooping down to the flowers below, twisting and somersaulting in the breezes.

White Butterfly brought everyone great happiness.

$\mathcal{E}$veryone believed White Butterfly was happy, even the garden's adored Lady Fairy. But secretly she had begun to long for wings of many colors. She thought they would be so much prettier – and others would admire her more. And the more she thought about what she didn't have, the unhappier she became. White Butterfly's preferred perch was a pine branch that hung over the garden lake. There, she began to spend long hours staring at her reflection and wondering how she could change her boring whiteness into lots of glorious colors. "I would do anything to change my color!" she often sighed.

"Hello, White Butterfly!" said Lady Fairy, interrupting her thoughts. The butterfly was very startled to see her.

"What's wrong with your color? Painters and children love the beauty of your silvery whiteness," commented the fairy.

"But right now, I have an urgent request – the Garden of Roses is in trouble. They need your help!"

"You are the only butterfly I know who can make the long, dangerous trip to save that beautiful garden." White Butterfly fluttered with pleasure at the compliment and darted to a willow branch to be closer to Lady Fairy. "This job is more challenging than any I have given you before. In the past, your strength, speed, and endurance were tested; now your cleverness and courage will be needed as well. Can you leave tomorrow?" asked Lady Fairy anxiously.

"Oh, Lady Fairy, I will gladly help… but…" stammered White Butterfly,

"Would you make my plain white wings beautiful, bright colors?"

Gently, Lady Fairy replied, "White Butterfly, is your request due to **vanity**?"

"Vanity? Is that bad, Lady Fairy?" replied White Butterfly.

"Well," explained the fairy, "We all have to ask ourselves if we just want to be prettier or better than anyone else, to show off, or pretend to be something we aren't meant to be. Vanity is when we are only interested in how we look on the outside without thinking about what we look like on the inside."

"It seems like such a small thing…" muttered White Butterfly.

"White Butterfly, we can talk more about that when you return." Lady Fairy's voice was urgent. "I am much more concerned about the big problem at the Garden of Roses." Then she paused…and sighed. "I'll grant your wish for different wings. But consider this; have you ever heard of the snow or the white roses getting tired of their color? Just imagine for a moment," continued the fairy, "how dull nature would be without the color white."

Receiving no answer, Lady Fairy sighed. "Let's meet here tomorrow morning and I'll give you directions for the trip," she said, spreading her shimmery wings.

White Butterfly was already in the Garden of Fragrance enjoying a breakfast of sweet nectar when the fairy arrived. "Lady Fairy, I'm ready to leave when you wish," she said, excited at the prospect of her upcoming mission. She darted into the sky, made a fast wide circle, and flew down in zigzags through the flowers, as if to assure herself of her own strength and speed.

"Good! Time is precious," replied Lady Fairy. "Although you have been in other risky places before, this trip will expose you to more dangerous situations. The Garden of Roses is dying because of a hateful spell cast upon it by Dark Fairy and her Ghostly Ravens. Because of your unique abilities, you will be able to bring much needed healing to the weakened flowers so they can grow strong again and push the evil spell out of the garden. Please listen carefully to my directions."

"The Garden of Roses is a few days to the south," said Lady Fairy, pointing to her map. "First, follow the long Valley of Daisies. Skim the clouds as you fly over Buffalo Mountain and Red Fumes River. Fly high or you might get dizzy! Next, follow Oak Hill; fly quickly – there is danger there! Then, you'll see...."

"I'll hurry as fast as I can!" interrupted the impatient butterfly. "I just want to come back soon."

"Remember," pleaded Lady Fairy, "it's important to stay rested. Without enough energy, you might have to turn back. But the flowers need your help! You must fulfill your mission."

"Now, you must leave. The entire Magical Realm will be with you on your journey."
White Butterfly stopped so suddenly her antennas got tangled. 'Magical Realm'?"

"My humble gifts come from the immense love that connects us all together.
That's the true essence of magic," replied Lady Fairy in a soft voice.

"But Lady Fairy, why do you call your gifts humble? You are not weak!"

"Humility doesn't come from weakness – it comes from our strength.
Humility keeps our souls tender and our minds clear and helps us
see at a glance who and what is truly meaningful in life. It
helps us to love ourselves and love others. When we
understand how we are all special beings, each with
unique and wonderful differences, we become
humble, without feeling a need to brag or change
our appearance."

White Butterfly thought about Lady
Fairy's words, but secretly, she still
longed for prettier wings. She would
show everyone just how special
she was – fast, acrobatic,
AND fabulously colorful.

"It's time to depart. Safe journey, White Butterfly. Thank you for your willingness to help!" With her soft brown eyes, Lady Fairy gazed lovingly at the small butterfly. White Butterfly perched on the fairy's arm, moved her antennas up and down, and soared into the cloudless sky.

As the sun's rays glinted off White
Butterfly's brilliant wings, they looked like white
petals being carried on the breeze. When she looked back, she
saw Lady Fairy getting smaller and smaller. The garden became a small
green patch, and then eventually disappeared.

Just as twilight was touching the shadows of night, White Butterfly arrived at the
Valley of Daisies. An ocean of cheerful flowers spread below her as far as she could
see. She settled in the top of a birch tree and slept soundly all night.

The next morning, as the sun painted the sky a radiant pink, White Butterfly continued
her journey. The sky was vast but her wings were strong as they beat against the warm,
soft air at a steady pace. She soared over forests and farmland, hurrying on and on
until the sun started to sink on the eve of the second day. Buffalo Mountain
was so close she could almost hear it snoring. And soon, she was snoring
along in perfect harmony. Early the next morning, heeding Lady
Fairy's warning, she steered clear of Red River's stinky
fumes, then soared on to Oak Hill.

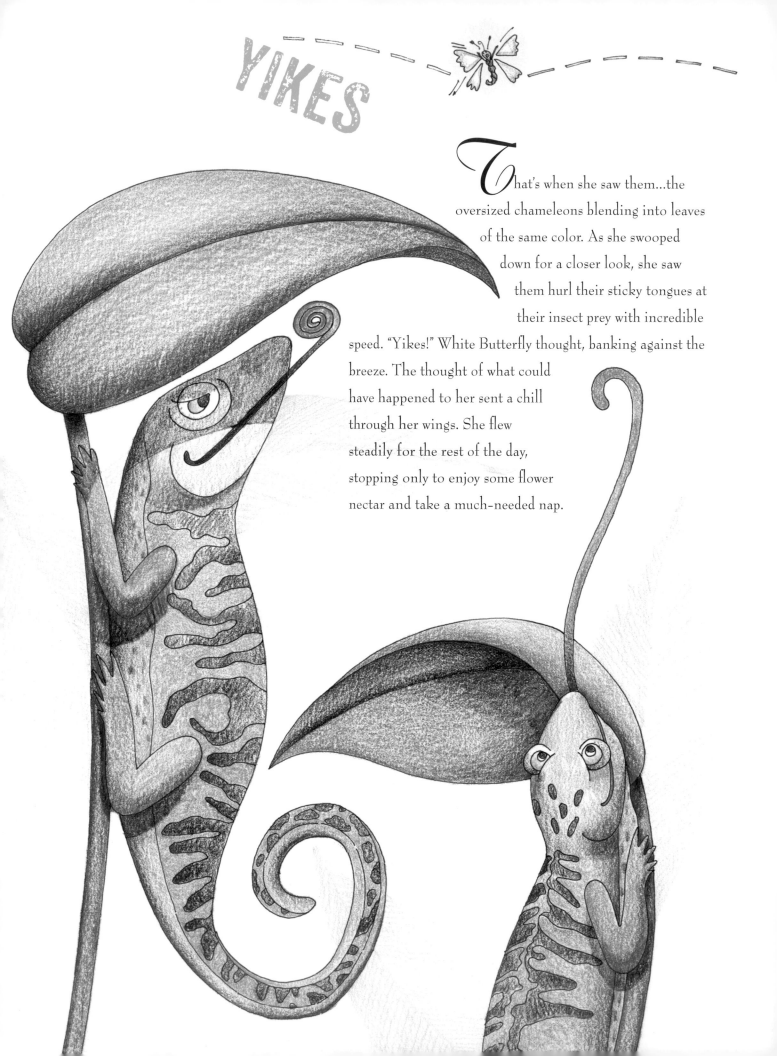

That's when she saw them...the oversized chameleons blending into leaves of the same color. As she swooped down for a closer look, she saw them hurl their sticky tongues at their insect prey with incredible speed. "Yikes!" White Butterfly thought, banking against the breeze. The thought of what could have happened to her sent a chill through her wings. She flew steadily for the rest of the day, stopping only to enjoy some flower nectar and take a much-needed nap.

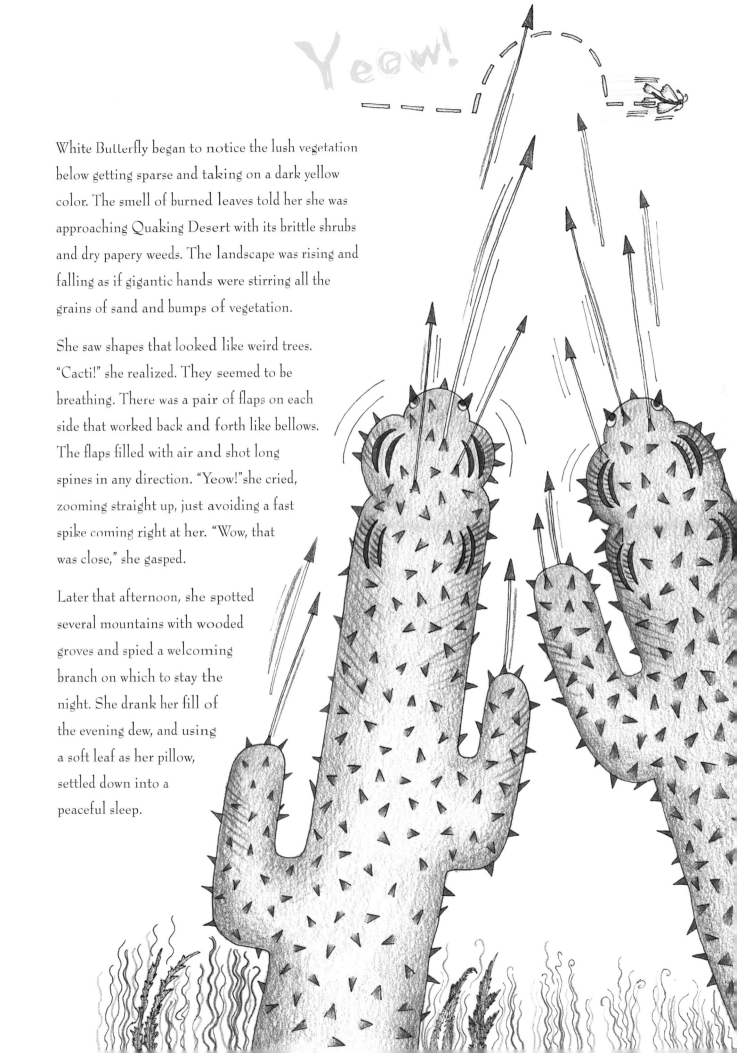

Yeow!

White Butterfly began to notice the lush vegetation below getting sparse and taking on a dark yellow color. The smell of burned leaves told her she was approaching Quaking Desert with its brittle shrubs and dry papery weeds. The landscape was rising and falling as if gigantic hands were stirring all the grains of sand and bumps of vegetation.

She saw shapes that looked like weird trees. "Cacti!" she realized. They seemed to be breathing. There was a pair of flaps on each side that worked back and forth like bellows. The flaps filled with air and shot long spines in any direction. "Yeow!" she cried, zooming straight up, just avoiding a fast spike coming right at her. "Wow, that was close," she gasped.

Later that afternoon, she spotted several mountains with wooded groves and spied a welcoming branch on which to stay the night. She drank her fill of the evening dew, and using a soft leaf as her pillow, settled down into a peaceful sleep.

$\mathcal{A}$s the woods came to life at the break of dawn, White Butterfly took off with great speed to continue her journey. Flying straight toward a plump cloud formation above, she leveled off and stayed on course over a wide valley, looking for the two lakes on her map. Finally, White Butterfly saw the first one — Flying Snakes Lake. Circling low, she heard a flute-like sound and felt a pleasant vibration hitting her body. She could barely resist the mysterious, paralyzing beauty of that bewitching sound, but FLASH! Lady Fairy's warning came back to her. The flying snakes became so excited that their whistling turned to a deafening shrill. Covering her ears, White Butterfly flew hard until she was beyond their reach.

outtahere!

$\mathcal{B}$ouncing on the current, White Butterfly darted on to Swans Mirror Lake. A pine-scented breeze gently ruffled the scales of her wings. She marveled at the lovely white swans, bathed in shimmering pink and blue shadows, gliding around the peaceful lake.

Enchanted by their delicate beauty, she happily continued south until the sun slowly slid behind Purple Mountain, where she stopped for the night.

Drinking in the early morning air, White Butterfly soon found herself above an astonishing valley embroidered with gardenias and daffodils. A delicious scent of thousands of flowers perfumed the air. She was amazed at the immense and colorful carpet of blossoms surrounding the cottage of Shining Fairy, the queen of the Garden of Roses.

Suddenly, White Butterfly gasped! Many flowers had browned edges and shriveled petals. The garden was indeed dying! Shining Fairy was waiting for her. "Look," she said in a choked voice, sadly pointing to the withering flowers. "If something is not done soon, they will be forever gone."

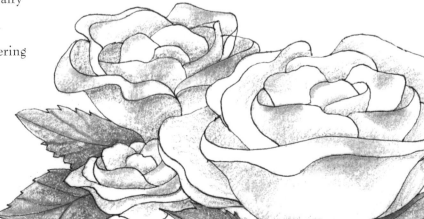

"How did this happen?" White Butterfly exclaimed. Shining Fairy sighed deeply. "The breeze, the rain, and all the garden's creatures were scared away by Dark Fairy and her Ghostly Ravens. Sometimes she and the ravens, on whom she cast an evil spell, travel through this region late in spring, spreading terror and desolation wherever they go. Their dark energy is growing faster than the flowers can push it away."

After a quick nap, White Butterfly got right to work. She dabbed her wings in the pollen of orange poppies and yellow daffodils, then in the sweet dew from spring beauties. She sprinkled her healing potion onto each flower, whisking her wings back and forth with incredible power. On each pass, White Butterfly filled the garden with light and healing. Strengthened by the potion, grateful flowers were happy to again be able to lift their heads and spread their leaves, pushing the evil spell out of their garden.

As White Butterfly made the last round over the golden sunflowers, Shining Fairy signaled the butterfly to perch on her extended arm.

"I can't thank you enough, White Butterfly! I have known many butterflies, but none have been so kind, strong, and courageous as you. Because of all your hard work, I shall give you a special gift," she exclaimed. "You have done your best." Shining Fairy asked the beautiful roses to kiss the little butterfly's wings. Instantly, White Butterfly felt as if her wings were made of rose petals, fragrant and soft!

"You will be the only butterfly who will always carry the delightful aroma of roses," said the grateful fairy.

White Butterfly was pleased with Shining Fairy's gift, but in her heart what she really wanted was her many colored wings.

*D*awn still had hazy patches of morning fog when White Butterfly prepared to leave. Flowers closed and opened their petals and swayed in perfect rhythm to bid her farewell. Shining Fairy again invited White Butterfly to perch on the palm of her hand. "Thank you – and go in peace," she whispered gratefully.

Those were the last words the butterfly heard as she zoomed straight up into the turquoise sky. The Garden of Roses slipped into the distance as White Butterfly rushed toward home on a steady breeze. She flew over Purple Mountain; she glided past Swans Mirror Lake, Flying Snake Lake, and Quaking Desert. She zoomed above Oak Hill, those stinky red fumes, past Buffalo Mountain, and finally, soared over the Valley of Daisies. She arrived back in the Garden of Fragrance in record time. She was HOME!

Lady Fairy was delighted to see White Butterfly return so soon. "Welcome back!…Umm, what a delicious rose scent you have," she exclaimed, her fairy eyes shining. "Tell me about your courageous trip."

"Well," White Butterfly spoke so fast her words tumbled forth like a rushing river, "My trip was perfect, thanks to your instructions…You should have seen the giant lizards… The flowers were strong when I left… Shining Fairy made me the only butterfly with a rose scent…and I flew hard so I could get home…fast…," she gushed breathlessly.

Lady Fairy was delighted with White Butterfly's success. But she noticed the little butterfly couldn't take her eyes off a small leather pouch hanging from her blue skirt. "Lady Fairy, does that bag have a potion for my colors?" White Butterfly asked in a tremulous voice.

Slowing nodding, the fairy carefully untied the magical pouch. "White Butterfly, I can't help but have a strange feeling about these new colors."

"Why, Fairy? Just because I prefer prettier colors to mine?" replied the puzzled butterfly.

"Yes…if you get tired of how you look now, you could get tired of how you look later on. Vanity is funny. It can be an endless craving for things that will become uninteresting as new things appear. You are already quite beautiful as you are," observed Lady Fairy.

White Butterfly rippled, spreading a rose aroma in the cool, twilight breeze, and perched on the edge of the yellow lily. "Lady Fairy," White Butterfly almost whispered, "I just know I will be happy with my new colors… forever."

"I hope so, White Butterfly, I hope so," Lady Fairy murmured as she finished the potion. "Now, please stand on that branch." White Butterfly shivered with excitement. With a willow twig, the fairy sprinkled White Butterfly three times. "White Butterfly, I have just granted the wish you have been yearning. In a few moments, you'll be seized by a deep sleep that will last until tomorrow."

White Butterfly's wings became so heavy that she hardly had strength to fold them before sleep overcame her. She became a small bundle of slumbering whiteness, blanketed by the moon's light.

The first sun rays darted throughout the Garden of Fragrance, and one diamond-like ray found its way through the leaves, lightly striking the sleeping White Butterfly. When she opened her eyes, she was startled by the streak of bright light so close to her. She flapped her wings and realized the glare came from the glowing colors from them! "Fairy! Lady Fairy!" she shouted excitedly. "Thank you for my colors!"

White Butterfly's happy voice echoed throughout the wood. But she heard no reply from the good fairy.

She rushed to the pine branch where she used to gaze at her white image in the dark green water. But she saw only a dark object vaguely mimicking her movements on the lake. "Oh, no! What happened?" The white image she enjoyed and pretended to chase around was no longer there. "My rose aroma is gone, too!" The butterfly's disappointment mounted. She had lost something about herself that she now realized she had truly loved. But it didn't take her long to remember that she was now the spectacular *Manycolor Butterfly.*

"Well, if I can't see myself on the lake, my friends will tell me if I'm really as striking as I want to be," she exclaimed, showing off her dazzling new wings.

White Butterfly's friends didn't recognize the strange, beautiful butterfly floating over the garden. Flower petals shook, confused and bewildered by her blazing colors. But Manycolor Butterfly only noticed that her colors made a big impression. She didn't see that her friends were now afraid of her.

Manycolor Butterfly just couldn't resist showing off. Human adults and children were also amazed by her dazzling colors and acrobatics. They followed her from branch to branch, charmed by her spectacular tricks and her unexpected color array.

Because she felt she had become so popular, Manycolor Butterfly extended her trips to gardens and parks farther and farther away. But the more shows she did, the less time she had for her own Garden of Fragrance.

"Ever since I granted you those colors, you have not been caring for your garden," Lady Fairy told her one evening. Manycolor Butterfly argued, "Lady Fairy, I haven't forgotten our garden. I'll be up bright and early in the morning, taking care of our home." She awakened to the cool dawn, thinking about her promise to the fairy. But she really craved the excitement of doing faraway shows and the admiration it brought her.

MORE!

more!

ahhh

"I'll work fast and get everything done so I still have time for other parks," she murmured. But hardly two hours had passed when Manycolor Butterfly started thinking about all the people in the neighboring garden calling for an encore of her last acrobatic display. "More, more!" her adoring crowd had chanted. She tried to keep doing her work, but she couldn't resist the attraction. So she rushed to the Park of Evergreen, leaving her care of the Garden of Fragrance incomplete. The garden flowers drooped their heads in sadness.

$\mathcal{M}$anycolor Butterfly had become the talk of the neighboring towns. Butterfly collectors gasped in amazement. One Sunday afternoon, the sun shone like it had been polished by the morning rain. People were everywhere, scanning the trees. Suddenly, children cheered.

"There she is! There she goes! Here she comes!"

Manycolor Butterfly executed a perfect graceful loop, then zoomed way, way up in a straight soaring line. Making a graceful turn, she came back in a fast nose dive and swung away just a few feet from the open-mouthed throng. Once above the crowd, Manycolor Butterfly zipped into an amazing, widening spiral, her wings shimmering in the sun. Again and again she thrilled the crowd.

But after so much frolicking, Manycolor Butterfly grew very weary. Zigzagging out of the spotlight to take a nap in a willow tree, she immediately fell asleep.

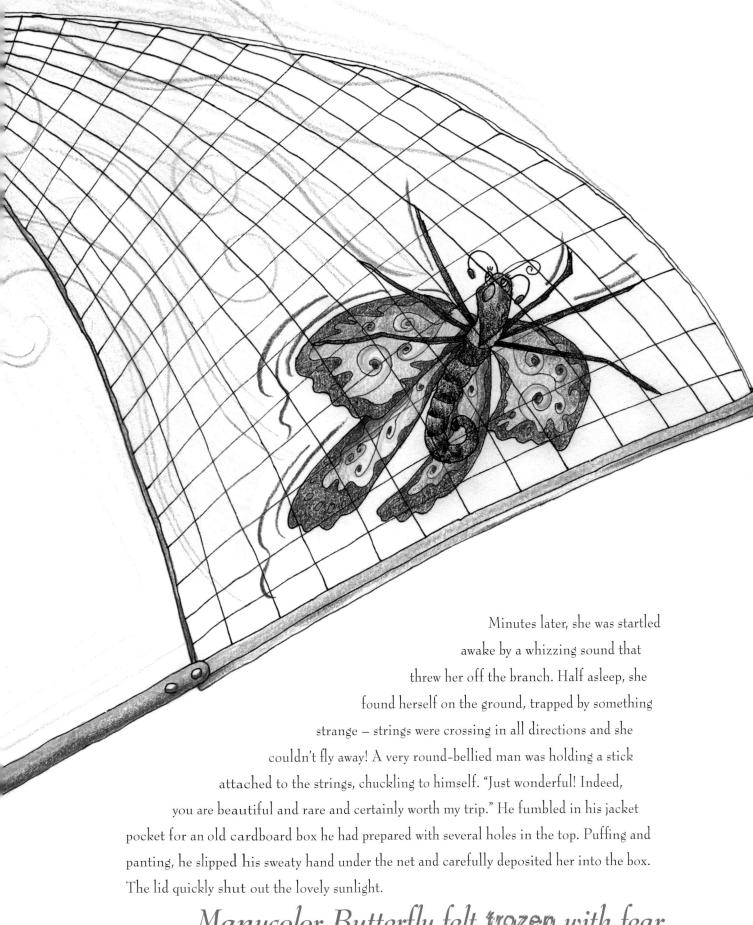

Minutes later, she was startled
awake by a whizzing sound that
threw her off the branch. Half asleep, she
found herself on the ground, trapped by something
strange – strings were crossing in all directions and she
couldn't fly away! A very round-bellied man was holding a stick
attached to the strings, chuckling to himself. "Just wonderful! Indeed,
you are beautiful and rare and certainly worth my trip." He fumbled in his jacket
pocket for an old cardboard box he had prepared with several holes in the top. Puffing and
panting, he slipped his sweaty hand under the net and carefully deposited her into the box.
The lid quickly shut out the lovely sunlight.

Manycolor Butterfly felt frozen with fear.

"Come on, don't be afraid," the admiring collector whispered. "I won't hurt you. You are not only beautiful, but also rare – your amazing colors and acrobatics – your strong body…." He knew she was a great catch. "I'd like to keep you in my own collection, but you will bring me sorely needed money!" The butterfly collector smiled at his luck, put the box in his pocket, and ambled to his car parked at the edge of the park. "I want to go back to my own garden!" she sobbed. The lure of admiration and fame had taken her far from home and brought her lots of attention. But she suddenly remembered Lady Fairy's warning – was her vanity the cause of all this trouble?

The roar of the car engine sent a shudder through her. Shortly, they screeched to a stop. The man rushed into his dining room where he kept a large, sparkling clear glass dome to inspect insects. Carefully, the collector snatched the exhausted butterfly from the box, lifted the transparent glass cover, and quickly released her under the dome. Manycolor Butterfly tried to fly free, only to strike against the glass again and again. The man let out an amused laugh at her frantic attempt to escape.

The butterfly collector had a round, glossy head and bushy eyebrows shooting in all directions. When he grinned, his thick, curly lips exposed his uneven, tobacco-stained teeth. His soiled clothes smelled like stale sausage. Yet he was quite enchanted with the butterfly's startling beauty and had an irresistible desire to hold her again. So he tilted the glass cover until there was just enough space for his pudgy hand to reach in…

…and just enough space for the desperate Manycolor Butterfly to escape from her crystal jail.

She soared to one of the cornices high up in the living room. "Oh, no!" cried the frazzled butterfly collector as he scrambled frantically after her! He yelled threatening words! He banged into chairs! And he rushed around searching for a soft cloth to trap her without damaging her wings.

Manycolor Butterfly was terrified!

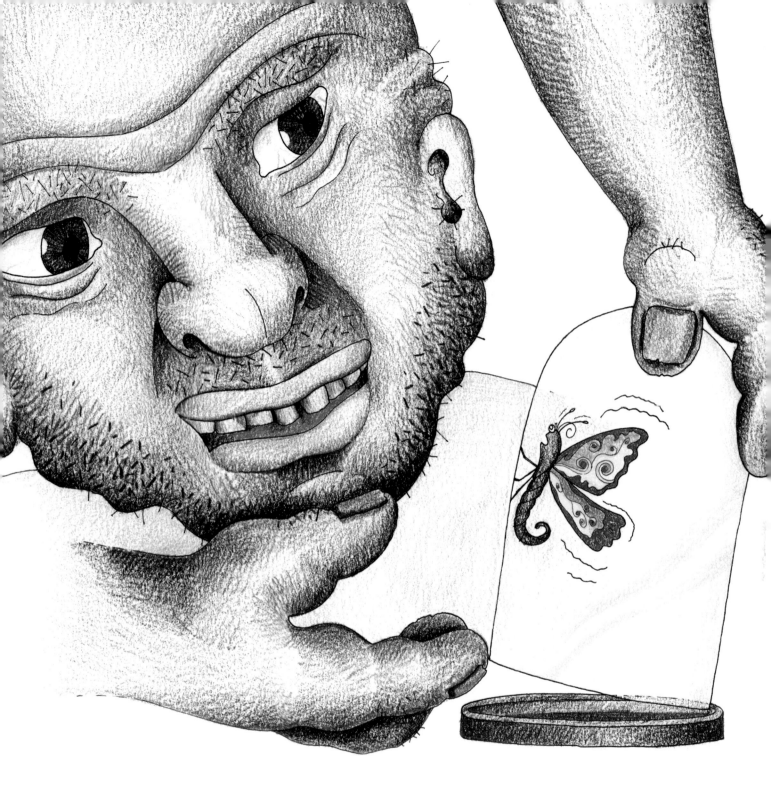

Seeing how high the butterfly had flown, his yelling changed to puffing and groaning.
She scanned the room for a crack to squeeze through to fly outside. And in her anxiety,
she could hear Lady Fairy's warnings in her head. But even though the butterfly knew
Lady Fairy believed in her, how could the fairy find her when she was so far away?

Tearfully, Manycolor Butterfly cried for help!

*M*eanwhile, the sweaty butterfly collector pulled the sheet from his bed, twisting it lengthwise. He quickly flicked the sheet, hitting her lightly, and she somersaulted upside down to the sofa. He grabbed her before she could escape.

"HA!" he gloated in a cracked voice. "I'll fix you. I will sell you for good money, no matter what." He rushed to a dusty cabinet, pulled out a drawer, and grabbed a battered tin box. He fingered noisily through half-chewed pencils, broken rubber bands, pointy buttons, pieces of dirty string, and some false teeth. He found just the pin he was looking for. Reaching for one of his own butterfly collections hanging on the wall, he prepared to pin her to an empty spot. But in his haste he neglected to secure one of her wings.

Courageously, Manycolor Butterfly made a huge, desperate shudder. The pin shook, stabbed through the thin tip of one wing...and also the man's finger! He screeched in pain, opened his hand, and she darted away, grateful for her wonderful gift of lightning fast speed. The little butterfly finally understood that her biggest error was not appreciating her true gifts.

Manycolor Butterfly asked for her pure white wings to be restored.

The man rushed into the kitchen for the ladder, bumping and banging it into the living room. But WHAT WAS THIS? The sight before him caused him to stop. The ladder clattered to the floor! He opened his mouth, but no sound came out. With eyes as big as saucers, he stared at a brightness that was flooding the whole room.

In its center was Manycolor Butterfly, surrounded by a glowing white circle. Her striking colors twinkled wildly, sparkling like millions of tiny stars, and then...melted away. The butterfly collector was dazzled by the sight of the most splendid white butterfly he had ever seen, radiating an exquisite brightness.

A sweet rose fragrance spread throughout the room as if thousands of petals had been crushed. The shabby living room had become a magical palace of light and aroma.

The butterfly collector stumbled; he was beyond surprise and amazement. "No, it can't be," mumbled the man, as one of the locked windows slowly opened, flooding the room with a brilliant blue beam. Somewhere, he heard a grateful voice saying, "Thank you, Lady Fairy! White Butterfly was perched on an astounding winged woman, dressed in a lovely gossamer gown.

"I knew what you were experiencing," said the fairy, her voice ringing like a chime from a crystal bell. "You were so focused on your new colors that you started to forget what makes you so beautiful – your heart, your helpfulness, your special skills, and your courage. Now you have learned what can happen when vanity becomes more important than your own self love."

"Oh, dear Fairy! You have given me back my own white color, and with it, I see your love as well. From now on, I will try to use my gifts in the best way I can," replied White Butterfly, her eyes brimming with tears.

The bewildered butterfly collector still couldn't believe what he was seeing. An insect changing color? Impossible! A fairy? Ridiculous! But seeing the fairy and butterfly glide through the window on a beam of light was even more unbelievable. When they had gone, his living room seemed even more shabby. The aroma of roses had been replaced by the smell of peeling wallpaper, the stench of cigar butts, and his sour, stained shirt. He staggered to the sheet and noticed small blood spots from pricking his finger. "So, I didn't just dream this. Oh, my! Who would believe me? I hardly believe it myself." The next day he sold his collection and never collected another butterfly again.

When everyone from the Garden of Fragrance saw their beloved butterfly returned to them, dressed in her brilliant white colors, they couldn't do enough to show her their joy. Expressions of love and admiration turned into a holiday of scents, sounds, and colors, accompanied by a choir of buzzing bugs and a parade of dancing flowers. White Butterfly, deeply moved and excited, sailed around in loops and spins to the amazement and amusement of all in the garden.

When she spread her wings, she noticed the little brown spot left by the rusty pin. "Lady Fairy, will this spot ever disappear?"

"As you become happier and happier with the you inside of you, it will gradually fade."

"Then, it will fade away soon, Lady Fairy, because I couldn't be happier – with me." With gratitude, White Butterfly raised and lowered her marvelous, luminous, shimmering white wings.